The Secrets
Of Code Z

Case #5

A Belltown Mystery

By
T. M. Murphy

J. N. Townsend Publishing
Exeter, New Hampshire

2001

Cover design by Sally Reed.

Logo design by Richard Fyler.

Author photo by Amy Hamilton.

Printed in Canada

Published by
   J. N. Townsend Publishing
   12 Greenleaf Drive
   Exeter, New Hampshire 03833
   800/333-9883
   www.jntownsendpublishing.com
   www.Belltownmysteries.com

ISBN: 1-880158-33-7

Acknowledgments

I'd like to thank some of Orville's best supporters: Emily Chetkowski, Michelle Gonzalez-McEvoy, Ernesto Gonzalez, Carol Chittenden, Janet Cox, Betsey Welton, Kevin Whelan, Christa Soderstrom, Jean Gannon, and Olivia Townsend Orovich!

For Lindsey Kempton:

Whom I met only once. It was a cold gray December day, but it was a meeting that warmed my soul and reminded me why I love to write for young people. I am forever grateful.

The Secrets of Code Z

Chapter
One

Snow. Snow. And more snow. It had been snowing in Belltown for close to a week. School had been cancelled for a record five days in a row! It was every kid's dream come true. Sure, we would have to make up the snow days at the end of the year, but we'd deal with it then. Right now, I was going to enjoy my freedom. I decided to take my Great Dane, Ophelia, for a walk along Breakers Beach. Or maybe I should say, she decided to take me for a walk! She galloped through the sandy snow at the edge of the shoreline while I tried to keep pace. Finally, she stopped to smell an overturned horseshoe crab, while I took the time to catch my breath and think about the wonderful day ahead of me. Friday morning and no school. Does it get any better than that? I suppose Monday through Thursday without school, but that had already happened. What was really going to make this day special was "Coté's World Famous Winter Carnival." It was Belltown's winter version of the county fair except this carnival was designed for the snow—snowmobile rides, sleigh rides, snowball throwing contests, etc. This was going to be the first winter carnival in Belltown in fifteen years so I think that's why the adults didn't even mind the snow. The more snow the better the carnival. I couldn't wait, though, because it was also going to be my first real date with Vanessa Hyde. We had gone sledding a couple of days before but that was during the day. This was going to be a night date. I didn't know how I felt about Vanessa, but I knew a night date at the fair would be a major test for both of us.

Ophelia brought me back into the moment as she almost ripped my arm out of the socket while following another scent. After being dragged twenty yards, I got a solid hold of her. She gave up and rested before the sign in front of the jetties. The sign read, "WARNING: NO LIFE-GUARD ON DUTY. PLEASE STAY OFF ROCKS." I brushed some snowflakes off my glasses with my glove and nodded in thought. Summer seemed only like it was yesterday and now it seemed so far away. It would be several months before I could go bluefishing, scuba diving, or even take a dip on a blazing July day. Ophelia must've had the same feeling of sadness as she began to bark like a rabid dog at the incoming waves smashing against the rocks. "Ophelia, I know you want to go for a swim, girl, but you can't. Now come on. Come on, girl." I pulled on her leash as she gave one last growl at the ocean before giving in to the tug. I told myself to forget about the sadness of summer being so far away and focus on the excitement of the carnival. Little did I know what kind of excitement I was in for.

Anyone who was anyone was waiting outside the gates of Coté's World Famous Winter Carnival. The place was absolutely packed and people were getting antsy considering it was 7:14 PM and the gates were supposed to open at seven. Just as I was about to ask Vanessa what she thought the delay was all about, there was a loud bang and suddenly blue and white fireworks colored the dark sky. Everyone clapped at the unexpected display.

"Ladies and gentlemen. Boys and girls. If you could please look above the main gate," the voice on the intercom requested, and all eyes shifted. A spotlight lit up a podium, which was above the gate.

"The people of Cape Cod, I proudly present the owner of Coté's World Famous Winter Carnival, Charles Coté, the third." The enthusiastic voice warmed the crowd.

The spotlight stayed focused on the podium but no one appeared. "You can't see Mr. Coté?" The man on the intercom asked.

"Then look above you to the right."

The spotlight shifted to the sky, where a skydiver waved down to the crowd. Green lights then lit up the podium. That's when we all realized the skydiver was going to attempt to land in the ten-foot circular area. There was silence for a minute until both his feet came down on the podium and he nailed a perfect landing. A loud cheer followed and I looked at Vanessa. Our eyes met and I thought about kissing her. The moment was right. She moved closer and my nerves jumped. The next thing I knew I was awkwardly putting my hand up to high-five her. She looked confused but high-fived me back and we both admitted,"That was awesome." Inside, I was scolding myself. Jacques, what's wrong with you, she's your date, not your teammate hitting the winning shot at the buzzer! But sometimes you do stupid stuff when you like someone. I wasn't going to dwell on it any longer.

The skydiver, who was wearing a white suit, collected his chute while the cheering continued and then he picked up a walk-around microphone.

"Thank you. Thank you." He waited for everyone to quiet down. "I'm sorry we're opening the gates a little late, but I got stuck in a head wind and you know how that can be during the rush hour."

There were a few laughs and a couple of groans.

"Maybe I shouldn't have opened with that one."

Everyone laughed at the honesty in his voice.

"Let me tell you a quick story. Well, when I was about four years old my Dad got lucky and made millions in the stock market. His dream wasn't to move to Florida. It was to play in the snow! At Coté's World Famous Winter Carnival we've been doing that ever since. We took a chance on *The Farmer's Almanac* this year. It said Belltown, Cape Cod, would be buried with snow. They were right. So, let's open the gates and play in the snow!"

The crowd roared as the gates opened and everyone inched inside the carnival.

"Orville, look at that." Vanessa pointed over to a full-sized ice sculpture of a unicorn.

"It's ... It's ..." I was trying to find the right word to describe the unicorn.

"Breathtaking." Vanessa summed it up.

"I'm glad you like her. Her name is Princess. She *is* a Princess, don't you think?" a voice said behind us.

Vanessa and I turned around and standing before us was the skydiver. He was probably in his early thirties. He had flaming red hair and a muscular build.

"Did you sculpt Princess?" Vanessa asked.

"I wish I had that talent." He shook his head.

"Well, it looks like you have other talents. That was quite a jump especially since you had no light," I said.

"Thanks." He smiled.

"What did you jump out of?" Vanessa asked. "I mean, I didn't hear an airplane."

"Actually, I jumped out of my buddy's chopper. The reason you guys didn't hear anything, we flew over when the fireworks were going off in the other direction."

"That's pretty impressive. But I'm not surprised, considering you were a paratrooper in the army," I guessed, trying to test my skills of deduction.

"Why do you say that?" His eyebrows raised.

"Orville!" Vanessa gave me a look and then turned to the skydiver, "Don't mind him. He's always trying to make connections."

She was right. It was something I learned from watching Magnum, P.I., reruns. Always practice deduction. Even when you're not on a case.

"I don't mind at all because he's absolutely right. Seventh Division Seventeenth Infantry Desert Storm, Colonel Charles T. Coté the third. But call me Chuck." He shook my hand.

"Orville Jacques the first. But, unfortunately, call me Orville." We both laughed.

"And who is your lovely girlfriend?" The word "girl-friend" hung in the air like a fly ball. Chuck sensed the tension and tried to catch himself. "I mean friend."

"Vanessa Hyde." Her blue eyes lit up as she shook his hand. A worker interrupted us. "I'm sorry Mr. Coté, but Hilda has to talk to you."

Chuck gave a look of concern and then whispered in the worker's ear. The worker nodded but he did not leave.

"If you will excuse me, Orville and Vanessa. It was a pleasure meeting you both." Seconds later Charles Coté, the third, was lost in the crowd.

"Well, here you go." The worker handed us two tickets that read "complimentary".

"What do these mean?" Vanessa asked.

"They mean food, rides, everything is on the house. Except for the games that is." The worker began to walk away.

"Why?" Vanessa and I were pleasantly stunned.

He pointed at me. "Because Mr. Coté said he liked your style." I was trying not to smile.

"I know you want to smile," Vanessa laughed.

"About what?" I shrugged and bit my lip.

To say it was turning out to be one of my best dates ever would be an understatement. Vanessa and I were having an absolute blast. We went on about fifteen rides and ate as much carnival junk food as we could swallow. I even won a teddy bear at the "hit the target with an iceball"

game. It was the first time I ever won anything at the fair. Naturally, I gave the bear to Vanessa. She loved it and suggested we take a sleigh ride through the woods. A romantic sleigh ride through the woods. I knew it couldn't get any better than that. And guess what, I was right! As I helped Vanessa get into the sleigh a voice stopped me.

"Do you have room for one more, Jedi?"

Jedi. There was only one person in the world who called me Jedi. It couldn't be, I thought.

"How are you doing, Jedi?"

It was! Joe Clancy, the thirteen-year-old Star Wars fanatic. I was stunned to see him because his family only summered in Belltown. He was sort of like a little brother to me, always following me around.

"Joe, what are you doing in town?"

"Could you hold this for me?" He handed Vanessa his candied apple and hopped into the sleigh and sat between us. So much for the romantic sleigh ride, I thought.

"You didn't hear, Jedi? We just moved down. I'll be living across the street from you year-round. Isn't that great?" He began chewing on his apple again.

"Yeah, great." I rolled my eyes.

The driver flicked the reins and we were off.

"Who's this?" Joe pointed at Vanessa.

"My name is Vanessa Hyde." She smiled and shook his free hand. "Oh, hi. I'm Joe Clancy. The Jedi has probably told you about me."

"He talks about you all the time." Vanessa was being a good sport. For the twenty minute sleigh ride, Joe talked our ears off from topics ranging from his favorite cereal to his favorite *Goosebumps* book that was about a green Jell-O ghost or something. Although I was annoyed that Joe had broken the romantic mood, I was happy to see him. He represented summer to me and it was good to see he hadn't changed one bit except for his clothes. It was the first time I had seen him in winter clothes. He was wearing a blue snowsuit with a Luke Skywalker patch sewn on it. When we got off the sleigh, he borrowed a dollar from me and scampered towards the concession stand in quest of a snow cone. Yup, Joe Clancy hadn't changed a bit!

"He's a cute little kid, Orville." Vanessa smiled at me.

"Well, he is one of a kind," I admitted.

"I can see he looks up to you. But, why wouldn't he? Considering you're such a great guy and all." Vanessa took my hand and stared into my eyes. I felt my face turning red. I was nervous and excited.

"Well, what do you want to do now?" I tried to remain cool.

"Well, what about that?" She pointed over to a wagon.

All my romantic thoughts left me when I saw the wagon. It wasn't just any wagon. It was a gypsy wagon, and I knew it wasn't just any gypsy who owned that wagon. It was the gypsy fortune-teller whom I had met the previous summer at the Belltown fair. That night, she had looked into her crystal ball and predicted unimaginable events for my future. I never put much stock in the supernatural stuff until her predictions came true to the very word. Her predictions actually helped me solve my first case. Whenever I couldn't sleep at night, a vision of her would often appear in my mind. I always wanted to ask her if she really had seen my future or was it just blind luck? Now, I was standing right outside her wagon.

"Well?" Vanessa looked at me as she ran her hand through her long blond hair.

"Well, what?" I had no idea what she was asking.

"Do you want to have our fortunes told?"

"Oh, yeah. I guess so."

"Are you OK, Orville?"

"Yeah, why do you ask?"

"'Cause, when you saw that wagon, it looked like you saw a ghost."

"No, I'm fine," I said as we approached the ticket-taker who stood in front of the wagon door. He was a giant of a man with black, unwashed hair and meat hooks for hands.

"Tickets," was all he said.

We handed him our passes and he hunched over and peered down at them for what seemed like a lifetime.

Finally, he said, "One at a time."

"Sir, can't we get our fortunes told together?" Vanessa asked politely.

"One at a time," he repeated and then pointed his thick finger at Vanessa. "You go first."

Vanessa looked at me a little bewildered.

"It's OK, Vanessa. I'll go after you," I reassured her.

"All right. I guess so," she said as she headed up the two steps that lead to the wagon door. Vanessa looked back at me. I knew the man had made her feel a bit uneasy.

"Find out if we're going to have any more snow days,"

I laughed. I was trying to lighten the moment and it worked. She chuckled a bit before opening the door and entering the wagon. My comment may have lightened the moment for Vanessa, but for me it was another story. For the next five minutes, I didn't even notice the cold temperature or anything for that matter. I kept thinking how I was going to approach the fortune-teller. I mean, would she even remember me? Probably not. I took off my gloves and noticed that my palms were clammy. My breathing felt heavy, too. Why was I getting so tense? I couldn't figure out my anxiety. I took a deep breath. "Calm down, Orville. You're freaking out over nothing."

"What?" The giant asked.

"Oh, nothing. I'm just talking to myself."

He grunted and went back to his blank stare while blocking the doorway again.

I was feeling a little better and began stretching when my eye caught something. On the side of the wagon, there was a small oval window with a curtain. A hand moved the curtain ever so slightly. I looked away pretending I didn't see anything. Someone was watching me from the wagon. I was positive. I decided to count to three and then look back again.

"One. Two. Three." My eyes raced over to the window and just caught a brief view. It was only brief but I knew who it was—the fortune-teller.

Suddenly, the wagon door flew open. "Orville!"

Vanessa skipped the steps and leaped to the ground almost colliding with the giant.

"What's wrong?"

"It's the . . . It's . . . the . . . fortune-teller." She pointed back at the wagon.

"Is she ok?" The giant and I asked at the same time.

"I don't know. I was telling her about my life and you and everything and she looked out the window at you and . . ."

"And what?" I pushed.

"Well, when she saw you she rushed out the back door."

The giant didn't wait for any more of what Vanessa had to say. He took off for the woods behind the wagon.

"Why did she leave when she saw you?" Vanessa wanted the explanation I couldn't give.

"I don't know. I really don't know."

"Well, we have to find her. She's an old woman and she's not dressed for this weather." Vanessa's worried look spoke volumes.

"Let's go." I grabbed her hand and headed for the woods behind the wagon.

Vanessa and I quickly realized the crescent moon that had lit up the fairgrounds was no match for the foreboding woods. The deeper we went, the more the moon was gobbled by mammoth oak trees. But we pressed on, pushing branch after icy branch aside until we were at the point where the trees had won their battle, smothering the moon completely and leaving us with no light and no sound except for a lonely owl calling from beyond the next fortress of wilderness.

"There's no way she came out this far," I said.

The owl called out again and we both jumped a bit.

"Yeah, we better go back before we get lost." Vanessa said.

"Good idea." She was right. It would have been fool-hardy to go any farther. We turned around and retraced our steps. We didn't say a word until the moon became visible and the silence of the woods was replaced with distant screaming kids on roller-coasters. The sight of the Ferris wheel darting up and down through the trees told us we were safe.

"I wonder where she went?" Vanessa broke our silence.

"I don't know. The other question is, where did that ticket-taker go? We saw him run into the woods, but we didn't bump into him in there."

"Yeah, I mean, it's not exactly Yellowstone National Park," Vanessa said as we walked out of the woods.

"The big question is, now what?" Vanessa asked.

"I was thinking we should go tell Chuck since he owns the carnival. He probably could tell us if the fortune-teller has some sort of condition and has run out before while reading a fortune. And if he doesn't know, it's just good to inform him," I said while looking at a scuffle near the cotton candy stand. Two kids were pushing somebody who looked familiar.

"Isn't that Joe they're pushing?" Vanessa asked.

"Yeah, wait here," I said, and bolted over to the cotton candy stand. I recognized the two kids immediately—Paul Miller and Craig Hampton. They were two of the biggest jerks Belltown had ever produced.

Miller had Joe by the neck and Joe's eyes were like saucers.

"You get tougher by the day, Miller. Picking on a little kid." My nervous anger was making me shake.

"What do you want, Jacques?" Miller stared me down.

"I want to know what's going on." I wasn't going to back down even if they both were stars on our football team. And they weren't stars for being small! They were built like brick houses! "If you must know, we were having a little fun with Looney Larry over there." Craig Hampton pointed over to Larry, a well-known homeless man from Belltown who was lying in the snow moaning.

"Are you OK, Larry?" I helped him up.

"I'll be OK." He wiped the snow off his sixty-plus-year-old frame.

"Those jerks kept pushing Larry to the snow and every time Larry tried to get up ..." Joe couldn't finish his sentence. Miller picked him up and threw him into a garbage can by the cotton candy stand.

"Now you can help Looney Larry collect cans," Miller laughed, and Hampton joined him.

"Why you!" I charged towards Miller but someone beat me to him. The body flew through the air and knocked Miller against the trailer of the cotton candy stand.

"You're a real tough guy!! Aren't you?" Vanessa yelled as she pushed Miller's face into the snow.

"Vanessa?" I said in shock. I guess I was so much in shock that I didn't see Craig Hampton's right hook that knocked me to the ground. He pounced on top of me and pinned both my arms with his legs. I was flailing away like a hopeless fish knowing I was trapped. He cocked his right fist but before he could unload on me someone pulled him off me, yelling, "Break it up! Break it up!"

The voice kept barking orders that I couldn't make out at first.

"Jacques, get up!"

I rose to my feet and groaned at the sight of Officer Coughlin standing and hitting the palm of his hand with his baton.

"Jacques, you, your girlfriend, and the little kid are outta here!" he snarled.

"But Miller and Hampton started it all. They were beating up Larry, and Joe tried to stop them," I protested.

"Larry who?" he snapped.

"Larry." I pointed over to Larry but he was gone. "Larry the homeless man was here a minute ago."

"He's right," Vanessa began.

"I didn't see him. All I saw was your girlfriend jump Paul. Now get outta here before I put all three of you in protective custody. I don't think your parents would enjoy coming down to the station and picking you up!"

He pointed his nightstick at the gates. I could see Vanessa was going to protest, so I gave her a look of this-is-not-the-time. We reluctantly left the fairgrounds as it dawned on me why Officer Coughlin threw us out instead of throwing out Miller and Hampton. Officer Coughlin was also the assistant football coach for the Belltown High Pirates. The star players for the Pirates were quarterback Craig Hampton and halfback Paul Miller. That thought should have angered me even more. But my mind was back on a more important subject—the fortune-teller. Why did she run away from me? Tomorrow I would have to find out . . .

Chapter
Two

I HAD BEEN tossing and turning in my bed for hours trying not to think about the fortune-teller. Think about something else, I yelled in my mind. Well, I could think about how I kissed Vanessa good night after I walked her home from the carnival but that didn't happen thanks to good ol' Joe Clancy who clung to our side every step of the way. I turned over and the vision of the fortune-teller and her wagon invaded my thoughts again. There had been something different about her wagon. Then it struck me that this past summer the wagon had a sign on it. What did it say? I wondered.

I suddenly remembered:"Hilda's Amazing Crystal Ball."

"Wait, wasn't Hilda the name of the worker who had to talk with Chuck Coté?" I propped up in my bed. Hilda, of course it was. I tried to make out the blurry red numbers on my digital clock. No chance. I reached down beside my bed and felt for my glasses. I put them on and the red blur came into focus. 1:02 AM. I thought for a minute. I had decided I would try to find out tomorrow why the fortune-teller had run away when she saw me. The clock flicked 1:03 AM. Technically it was tomorrow. I pushed the covers off and hopped out of bed. In the past, I'd probably have had a tough time sneaking out of the house, but my room wasn't *in* the house. A few weeks before, my Mom had the old garage behind our house winterized and reno-vated into a small apartment and told me I could have it as my own place with the condition I'd use it responsibly. Sneaking out in the middle of the night probably didn't fall under her definition of responsible, I thought, and hesitated. I paused as I put on my clothes and felt even more guilty knowing Mom relied on me to set an example for my little brother, Billy, and little sister, Jackie, especially since Dad was still away on a teaching sabbatical in Ire-land. But then I thought of the fortune-teller again. I couldn't come to grips with the fact that she felt it was safer to run into the cold dark woods than to speak with me. What fear drove her away? I erased the guilt from my mind and finished dressing. The carnival may have been closed for the night, but I still had a ticket for my fortune to be told. Little did I know what that fortune would mean to the fate of the world!

Curiosity—the urge that I've never been able to fight—gripped me as I trudged along the snow-covered road. There were no streetlights and the crescent moon had been blocked by snow clouds. The night was black except for the faint glow my flashlight was able to cast on the blinding snow falling wherever the slashing winds threw it. I chewed on a piece of gum furiously to avoid shivering. I knew if I let one shiver invade my body, it would be contagious, and it would probably get to the point where I would turn around and go home. I couldn't do that. I had gone two miles and I only had one more to go. I figured if I waited for a civilized hour to go to the fairgrounds, the fortune-teller might either still be hiding from me or might even be gone. Then nothing would be solved. My questions would still be unanswered and the burning curiosity would still exist, and it was that curiosity that kept me warm while walking that last mile.

When I reached the fairgrounds, I flashed my light quickly to confirm what I had already expected: the gates were locked. But what surprised me was that there were no lights on outside the gates. In fact, I couldn't see any lights on anywhere. The grounds were pitch black, and the only thing keeping me from getting in was a twelve foot chain-link fence. This is easy enough, I thought, as I turned my flashlight off and went over to the fence. I pulled my gloves off and stuffed them and my flashlight into my coat pocket. At first touch, my fingers almost froze to the icy links. I knew I had to climb fast. I never was a good climber when it came to the ropes in gym class, but I could always climb fences well. I had a lot of practice sneaking into the high school football games when I was a little kid. I was relying on that practice as I slowly made it up the fence. The only problem was I had never climbed a fence wearing boots. I was inches from the top when my feet lost their grip causing my arms to do all the work. Go faster, I urged myself as I lunged for the top links and somehow pulled my body to the top of the fence. I had heard a sound and was only able to place it when I realized I couldn't move. The pointed links on the top of the fence had ripped through my snow-pants and I was stuck. I was glad I was wearing jeans underneath or they could have ripped through something else! I was going to have to wiggle myself out of my snow-pants, and it was probably going to take me a couple of minutes, but I was just relieved I was going to make it all the way over unscathed. At least, that's what I thought until I heard the sound of barking dogs. I gasped hard. I knew it wasn't excited dogs playing in the snow. These barks were vicious.

"Guard dogs," I blurted to myself as I tugged on my snow-pants. Forget the fortune-teller, I thought, get loose and get back on the other side. The barks got louder and louder as I pulled harder and harder and suddenly the pants ripped. It happened so quickly that I lost my balance and fell over slamming into the fence. I realized I was still dangling upside down in the air. I pulled out my flashlight and flashed it up at my right pant leg which was still stuck to the fence. I had fallen so fast that I didn't know which side of the fence I was on. The barks were louder than ever and from my upside-down view I pointed the light into the night hoping it wouldn't catch sight of anything, but it did. There were two four-legged shadows running my way, barking wildly. In a frenzy, I shook my leg and the final rip catapulted me to the ground. I jumped to my feet. The barking had stopped, but I heard something else above the howling wind. I didn't want to, but I had to flash the light at the sound. I was praying I was wrong about the sound, but I wasn't. The sound I had heard was a low growling. As I flashed the light, the growling became more fierce and I almost fainted at the sight of two saliva-spitting Doberman pinschers standing five feet away. I knew they were about to attack. I had to do something quick. But what?

I wish I could tell you that I had dog biscuits in my coat pocket or thought up some elaborate plan to distract the Dobermans while I made a run for it. But I didn't have any biscuits, and my mind wasn't working when it came to plans. I was too petrified as they cautiously inched closer and closer licking their fangs while snarling up at me. I snapped my head back and forth as I shined my light, surveying my surroundings. I spotted a circus-style tent ten yards to my left. A bottom portion of the tent's canvas was flapping in the wind. I could see a piece of rope dangling at the end of the canvas. It must've blown loose, I thought, leaving a small opening. That small opening was my best bet, my only bet. I broke for the tent like a base runner trying to steal second, and the barking began again. They were right on my heels, but I had one slight advantage—I knew where I was going. I slid face-first across the snow and through the opening of the tent. I leaped to my feet and saw the dogs were almost at the opening. In one motion, I grabbed the loose canvas and pushed it down and retied the rope to a stake in the ground, closing the entrance. The Dobermans were madder than ever, but their barks were now only threats.

"Wow. That was too close!" I shook my head.

"They're trained to put teeth marks in legs, but they're not trained to kill. Unless I tell them," said a voice in the dark. I almost fell over.

I turned my flashlight on and waved it around the tent. "Who's there?"

There was no answer.

"I said, who's there?" I tried to sound tough, but it was all acting.

"Me, that's who!" the voice whispered in my ear.

A second later, I felt a bearlike grip on my neck. I shined the light behind me and was able to make out the giant ticket-taker who had been outside the fortune-teller's wagon. His eyes were glowing like a man possessed, but right as I thought he was going to kill me, he let go and threw me to the ground. I coughed hard for a minute while massaging my throat with my right hand.

"You stay away from Hilda. Do you understand?" He flashed a light into my eyes.

"I will," I couldn't believe I was about to say this, "when I find out why she ran away from me."

"No," he yelled, "she's afraid of you. Stay away from her or I'll get the dogs! And I will!!"

"But why is she afraid of me?" I yelled back.

"No more questions!" He waved his hands in disgust.

"It's all right, Maxwell. You tried, but it looks like we can't discourage this young man." A female's voice came from the darkness. A flickering light then appeared. It came closer and closer until I could see it was a flame from a candle. Behind the candle was the old woman I had met the previous summer—the fortune-teller.

"Hilda, you should be resting. Go back to your wagon," the giant softly ordered.

"I wish I could rest, but I know our friend here will keep asking of questions. I of all people should know better than to try and run from fate." She sighed behind her gypsy scarves.

"Why did you run ..." I began.

"Sssh," she admonished, putting her index finger to her mouth. "Let us at least have the warmth of the wagon before I answer your questions. I will answer them all. And when I'm done answering your questions," she paused, "you might wish I had not."

"Would you want somesing hot to drink to warm up?" Hilda asked from behind a curtain, which I guessed was where her living quarters were. I was also trying to guess what her accent was. German or Russian?

"Yeah, I'll drink anything hot." I blew on my hands while staring at the mystical crystal ball on her table, wondering what information it held.

"I know you Americans like coffee but I do not have any. I hate the stuff. I can give you a cup of tea or chicken broth."

"Tea is fine. I'm not a big coffee fan myself."

A moment later, the curtain slipped open and Hilda appeared holding a tray with a steaming pot of tea. She placed the tray on the table beside the crystal ball, making it look not-so-mystical. I think she must've read the reaction on my face. "Do not worry about the crystal ball. That is not where I read the fortunes."

"Then where do you read them?" I asked before taking a sip and savoring it.

"I see a person's future …" she paused and tapped her wrinkled index finger against her forehead, "here. That is where I see the future. The crystal ball is just a … how you say it? … a gimmick for the fair."

She took a long sip while keeping her eyes on me. When she finished, she turned to the curtain. "Maxwell, I know you are behind the curtain. Please to go outside and wait until we are done talking. I will be OK."

There was no answer, just the sound of a door being shut.

"Maxwell is a good man. He has no family except for the carnival people, and he looks to me as a mother figure. But we are not here to talk about my relationship with Maxwell. Are we, Orville?"

"How do you know my name?" I sat up in my chair.

"I know more about you than I want to know, Orville. When I vork at carnivals and fairs reading fortunes in my crystal ball, I always make somesing up, somesing that will make the customer to feel happy."

"You mean you really can't see someone's future?" I was confused.

"No, I can, but I can only see their future if I touch them or a piece of their clothing. That summer night when you came to have the fortune read, I was going to give you the same happy story. But, unfortunately, my leg brushed against your leg. You see, I touched you, Orville, and I was forced to see some of your future. Things I could not believe. I had to make a decision to tell you the truth or not to." Hilda stopped to fill our cups.

"And you told me the truth, well at least a riddle that I figured out and it helped me solve my first case. So what's wrong with that?"

"Would you have taken on more cases if you did not solve that first one?"

I thought for a minute, "To tell you the truth, probably not."

"That is my point. My prediction in the summer has put you in danger many times and now..." Hilda trailed off.

"What?" I exclaimed as I put my teacup down.

"Once I have touched a person sometimes more information about their future vill come to me later in life. I had a vision that you were coming to the carnival tonight and I asked Mr. Coté if I could have the night off. He begged me to work since it was opening night. He has been so good to me. I could not say no. Well, when you came to the wagon it was then I had another vision of you."

"What was it?"

"It was blurry but I knew it would involve more danger for you. I made the mistake of telling you the truth before, so there is no use lying to you now. Give me your hands, Orville."

I put my shaky hands into Hilda's cold, purple palms.

She closed her eyes, "Yes, I have a vision. It is still foggy, but much clearer then before. There is an animal trying to show you somesing. I cannot make this animal out."

"Maybe it's one of the Dobermans," I suggested.

"No, I do not think so. I see somesing else. I see rocks. They are like boulders. The animal is still trying to warn you. It could be a horse because it is so big. I do not know. It is not very clear."

"A horse? I don't know any horses in Belltown," I said. This was going nowhere.

"Wait, wait, you're standing by a sign. I can only make out some of the words. Warning. Duty ... Stay ... Rocks."

Warning. Duty. Stay. Rocks. My mind was putting the pieces together. Then it clicked. "WARNING: NO LIFE-GUARD ON DUTY. PLEASE STAY OFF THE ROCKS," I blurted, thinking it must be a sign from a beach on the Cape. But which one? They all have those signs.

"Yes, I can see it now. Yes, yes, that is exactly what it says. I see an animal trying to jump into ..."

"An ocean." I guessed the end of the sentence.

"Yes."

"I get it. That's my Great Dane, Ophelia. She's as big as a horse!"

"OK. OK. Now that makes sense. Yes. Yes. I now see she is on leash. Your dog is trying to show you somesing in the water. But you will not listen to her."

It sounded just like what happened at Breakers Beach yesterday morning. It had to be Breakers Beach, but that was the past. Wasn't Hilda supposed to see my future?

"The vision is changing. It is dark and now you are walking on the rocks. I see the rocks clearer now. They are not boulders. They are jetties. Yes, you are walking along the jetties. You see somesing in the water and ... and ... and ... I am sorry. That is all I see." Hilda opened her eyes and looked at me, frustrated.

I took a sip from my cup and put it down quickly. "Thank you, Hilda."

"Where are you going?"

"I'm going to make your last prediction come true." I headed for the door and began to open it.

"Orville, one more thing. I did not run from you this evening just because I did not want to see your future."

"Then why did you run?"

"Sometimes, I do not only get visions of a person's future, but I also get *feelings* about their future. I got a feeling vhen I saw you tonight. A terrible ... vibration."

"What was it?" I took my hand off the knob.

"Death surrounds you, Orville. Death surrounds you."

Chapter
Three

"DEATH surrounds you." The quote pounded in my head as I stood outside the fairground's gates contemplating going home. I glanced at my watch: 4:16 AM. and three miles to go. But it was only a mile or so to Breakers Beach. I came to the fork in the road where I would have to make a decision. If I went right I would be heading home, where my warm bed was waiting. If I went left I would be heading to Breakers Beach where who knows what was waiting. I decided to flip a quarter. Heads, go home. Tails, go to Breakers Beach. I snatched the quarter out of the air and slapped it to my wrist. Heads.

"Heads. That means go home. But, would I really get any sleep?" I asked myself. I knew the answer. No. The curiosity would be driving me crazy. They say, "curiosity killed the cat." But, they also say, "a cat has nine lives." I was going to put my money on the last phrase, and hope this cat had a few more lives left! And speaking of left, I took it. I know what you're thinking: What is he, crazy? And you're right! Part of me was kicking myself saying, "Go home, you fool."

But the other part of me, the part that I can't explain, couldn't resist uncovering the unknown. That didn't mean I wasn't scared or tentative, because I was! In fact, it took me about ten minutes to realize I was walking at a snail-like pace. I picked up the pace and began a light jog and only stopped when the cries of gulls and the salty taste in the snow-blown wind told me I was at Breakers Beach.

"OK, Orville, be calm now," I told myself, trying to slow my rising heartbeat. I waved my light around until it found the steps leading to the beach. I treaded slowly down clutching one hand on the railing and the other on my flashlight until I reached the snow-covered beach.

Where do I go now? I wondered trying to remember exactly what Hilda had predicted.

Her voice spoke in my head. "It is dark and you are walking on the rocks. I see the rocks clearer now. They're not boulders. They're jetties."

There were five sets of jetties on Breakers Beach but Ophelia had barked at only one set. I happened to be standing directly in front of those jetties.

"No use in stalling," I told myself as I lowered my light to the ground and stepped on the first rock, almost losing my balance in the process. My muscles tensed. I had to be extra careful or I'd end up in the icy surf that echoed beyond the darkness waiting to paralyze my body. I shuddered thinking about the other times I had fallen into raging oceans and how I barely made it out. And because of it, drowning had become one of my biggest fears. I often wondered in the late hours when I couldn't sleep if drowning someday would be my destiny.

Take it easy, Jacques. You're on the rocks. Nothing to worry about, I whispered to myself. I felt like Indiana Jones in *The Last Crusade,* slowly stepping from rock to rock and sighing in relief after each successful attempt. When I reached the halfway point I stopped and directed my light to the ocean, to my left and then to the right. I didn't see anything except for the angry winter waves crashing against the rocks, shooting up sea spray in my path. I was about to continue when I thought I heard a noise behind me. I froze and strained my ears above the squawking gulls and the ocean's chorus. There it was again, I thought, someone is behind me. I jerked my body around and flashed the light at the sound. I jumped at the sight before I realized what it was—a sea gull eating some shellfish. The gull glanced over at me before returning to his early morning treat. I lowered my head and shook it, laughing lightly at how stupid I was acting when I saw something else—footprints. I gulped because I knew they had to be fresh prints since it had been snowing all night. I crouched down to make out the size of the print when a strange urge made me flash my light back to the ocean. I waved the light and this time I spotted something in the waves. I couldn't quite make it out as the whitecaps tumbled over it. Could these footprints belong to whoever is riding in those waves? I wondered. *Someone fell off the jetties and is drowning*, my mind screamed. Whatever it was, the waves were pushing it closer to the rocks. I had to do something. I looked around frantically trying to find something that I could use to pull whatever it was closer to me. I finally found a piece of driftwood. I hurried back to the edge of the rocks remembering I had to be careful or I could fall in. I leaned over and stretched for the object. It was just out of reach when a wave knocked it closer and it caught my driftwood. It was close enough for me to see some of it—clothing.

"Oh, my God!" I said, knowing that whoever it was, probably was dead. There was no way they could be underwater that long and survive.

"Come on! Come on!" I tugged the driftwood as hard as I could until it was a foot in front of me. I threw the driftwood to my right, and crouched catcher-style teetering on the edge. I grabbed the clothing with both my hands and my adrenaline did the rest. I pulled the clothing up hoping the person was still conscious. But what I saw made me forget about keeping my balance. I fell forward in fright and plunged into the ocean leaving the sounds of the beach behind and being greeted by the deathly silence below the waves. I struggled with the object, trying to get loose from it but somehow it was stuck to me. I couldn't tell where because I lost my glasses in the fall. I was finally able to surface, and that's when I let out my cries of horror.

"Help! Help!" I screamed to the empty beach, expecting no one to return my calls.

"Put your hand out!" a man's voice yelled.

A light shined in my eyes.

I must've put my hand out. I don't exactly remember. It happened so quickly and I was out of control.

"Stop yelling! I've got you!" The man pulled me and whatever was caught to me onto the rocks.

"Oh, my God! Oh, my God!" he said at the sight.

I ripped the clothing that was stuck to my coat zipper and was finally free of it. I unzipped my coat pocket, reached in and grabbed the quarter, and pressed it into his hand.

"Call 911! Call 911!"

The man was a blur but I think he nodded because he hopped from rock to rock and took off.

I knew 911 wouldn't make a difference, because there lying next to me smiling with a full set of teeth was a skull ...

"You're still shivering. Are you sure you don't want another blanket?" Officer Jameson asked as he slid back into his cruiser and sat beside me.

"No, thanks. I'm practically dry thanks to your heater." I forced a smile. The truth was, I was completely dry. I was still shivering for another reason—it's not every day I fall into the freezing ocean trying to save a skeleton! It had been almost two hours, but the memory still had me spooked.

"OK." Officer Jameson took out his note pad. "I'd like to go over your statement one more time."

"One more time and then could someone drive me home?" I was getting annoyed because we had already gone over my statement three times.

"Orville, I know you'd rather be talking to Detective O'Connell and the fact is, I wish you were talking to him.

But he's in some remote cabin in Vermont enjoying his vacation, and I'm stuck here with a John Doe skeleton. So bear with me, will you?"

Officer Jameson gave me a look I could read. He was nervous, and I really couldn't blame him. He had some big shoes to fill when it came to replacing my mentor and friend, Detective Shane O'Connell. Next to Shane, Officer Jameson was one of the few good guys on the Belltown police force, so I decided to lighten up.

"Sorry, Officer Jameson. I'm just a little testy because of everything. Go ahead."

"Thanks. I understand," he said, and peered down at his pad. "OK, you said you couldn't sleep so you decided to take a walk. Orville, I have to stop right there. With your track record, are you sure you're not working on a case?"

I looked Officer Jameson straight in the eye. "The truth is I've had a lot of trouble y'know with school and girls, and I couldn't sleep. I wanted to take a walk and clear my head. I know it probably sounds bizarre to you." I lied and he bought it.

"No, it's not bizarre at all. Orville, it wasn't too long ago I was your age." He gave an understanding smile before looking down at his pad.

"OK, you found fresh footprints and then you spotted something in the ocean. You grabbed it and fell in." He flipped pages. "The part I don't understand is that you can't describe the man who pulled you out?"

"I told you, without my glasses I'm as blind as a bat. I would have tried to squint or something if I knew he was going to take off after he called 911," I said as I looked out the window at the beach. Although everything was blurry, I was still able to make out the pink sun peeking in the east.

A tap on the driver's window interrupted Officer Jameson. He rolled the window down. "Yeah, whatcha' got?"

"We found this flashlight in some dunes over by the pay phone." The officer showed Jameson a plastic bag containing a flashlight.

"That's mine. I think I put it beside me when I was trying to pull that thing in. The guy who rescued me must've used it." I reached for the bag.

"Sorry, Orville that's evidence now. That flashlight probably has our mystery rescuer's prints on it. Good work, Warner." He rolled the window back up.

I couldn't remember if the rescuer was wearing gloves or not when he pulled me out, but I thought it was highly unlikely that he wasn't wearing them considering the weather conditions. But I kept my lips shut. I didn't want to rain on Officer Jameson's parade.

"Now another thing," Officer Jameson began before he spotted two cars approaching. "Well, it's about time," he muttered under his breath as he got out of the car.

"Who's that?" I asked.

"Stay here for a minute." He slammed the door.

The vehicles parked right next to the cruiser. I couldn't make out the color, but they looked bigger than cars. Maybe they were SUVs, I thought. Three men got out of one car and two men got out of the other. My blurry vision wasn't able to make out their faces, but I could see they were all in plain clothes. I thought that was strange especially since Belltown had only one detective and he was skiing in Vermont. They had been talking to Officer Jameson a while when I decided to lean over to the driver's side and push the power window button to hear what was going on. It was just dark enough that they wouldn't be able to notice the window was down.

"So that's all this Orville Jacques said?" one of the men asked Jameson.

"Yup. This might sound crazy but this kid has helped solve some murder mysteries before and I can't help but think that he's not telling the whole truth."

"No, it doesn't sound crazy," said the same man. "We've heard a lot about this kid. I'll have one of my men watch his every move. Now we'll take over from here. Where are the remains?"

"Wait, what about Orville?" Officer Jameson asked.

"What do you mean?" the man shot back.

"I thought you'd want to talk to him so I've been stalling. He's waiting in my cruiser."

"What! Get that kid out of here, now!" the man snapped.

"But I thought you'd want to talk to him since he was the one who found the remains?" Officer Jameson sounded confused.

"No! We don't want anybody to know we're here. I thought we made that point clear to your chief. Nobody is to know we're here. YOU GOT THAT, OFFICER JAMESON!" The man talked down to him as though he were a fool.

"Yeah, I've got it." Jameson nodded and headed back to the car.

"You gotta love those small town cops," one of the

other men said sarcastically, and Officer Jameson froze for a second contemplating turning around. He didn't. At that point, I realized I'd better put the window up. I pushed the button as fast as I could hoping the harder I pushed the faster the window would go up. It didn't. Officer Jameson was too close. I had to move back into my seat and hope he didn't notice it was still open a crack. I guess he didn't notice because he paused before opening the door and mumbled to himself, "Boy, do I hate the CIA."

My body was starving for sleep and I was so tempted to jump right into bed, but I had to look something up in my dictionary first. CIA, short for Central Intelligence Agency. I had heard the term used many times in countless movies, but what was the Central Intelligence Agency?

After flipping for a minute I found the definition and read it out loud: "CIA (Central Intelligence Agency) founded in 1947, the American agency responsible for the combined tasks of worldwide intelligence gathering and counterintelligence abroad." I placed the dictionary back on my desk and was even more confused than ever. Why was such an important government organization investigating a body found in Belltown? I had to find out, but first I really needed to get some sleep.

I sat on the edge of my bed tugging on my coat zipper. It was an eerie feeling when I realized why the zipper was stuck. A piece of cloth was still jammed inside the zipper's teeth.

I pulled the fragment of black material loose and examined it. That shiver went up my spine again when I thought how that small piece of cloth once belonged to someone who once had a life, family, and friends, but now was just a skeleton without a name. I threw the piece of cloth into my wastebasket and then fell into bed. As my eyes got heavy, I wondered who the mystery man was who rescued me, and why did he flee the scene? I also wondered about Hilda, and if she would have more visions about my future. Then I thought about the CIA again. Was there an agent outside my window watching my every move? But the last thing I thought about as my eyelids began to give up the fight was, who was the skeleton without a name? I pulled my blanket closer and decided to enjoy my nap because I had a feeling I wouldn't sleep again until all my questions were answered.

Chapter Four

"JEDI, ARE YOU going to sleep the day away?" A voice invaded my head. I must be dreaming, I figured.

"Come on, Jedi. Wake up."

Joe Clancy waking me up. What a lousy dream to have. Maybe this dream will lead into a better one, I hoped.

"Don't make me put this snowball down your shirt to get you up."

Snowball. The word triggered consciousness. I opened my eyes and realized it wasn't a bad dream, just a bad sight—Joe Clancy was sitting at the foot of my bed chomping on a snowball.

"Joe, how did you get in here?" I rubbed my eyes.

"Your mom unlocked the door for me. She told me it was about time you got out of bed. Wow, it's pretty cool what they did to this place," he said as he looked around. "Your mom says you call it 'The Shack.' How long have you been living in here? I mean, you weren't living here last summer." He took another bite of his snowball.

"Joe, what do you want?" I had a headache from lack of sleep.

"Remember all of us were going to go sledding down the Heights Hill at nine?"

"No, I don't remember. And who's all of us?"

"You, me, and Vanessa."

"Vanessa? I don't remember any of this."

"I guess so, that's why she sent me to get you. She's at the hill waiting for us."

"Aww, man." I fired the covers off, leaped out of bed, and grabbed my spare set of glasses.

"Joe, can you tell Vanessa I'll be there in ten minutes? I'm starving. I need to have a bowl of cereal or something."

"You want a bite of my snowball? It's really good. I poured maple syrup all over it."

I glanced at the half-eaten snowball and saw that it was a light shade of brown. It made me want to gag!

"No. I'll stick with Cap'n Crunch. Thanks."

"No problem. I better tell her you'll be twenty minutes though." Joe waved his hand in front of his face.

"Why?" I asked.

"You really need a shower. You smell like you were swimming at Breakers Beach or something."

The Belltown Heights ball park was right up the street from my house. In the summer, the park was always filled with kids either playing pickup games on the basketball court or baseball on the Little League field. On this day there were no signs of life except for two people waving at me from the top of the hill. I waved back and picked up the pace. For a second, I couldn't believe how I had forgotten about my sledding date with Vanessa. But then a flash of me struggling with the skeleton went off in my mind. I realized that after that horror, I was lucky just to remember my name! I was halfway up the hill when I thought of something else and stopped dead in my tracks. "I'll have one of my men watch his every move," the CIA official had said. I searched the park with my eyes to see if that was the case. I didn't spot anyone, but then again, I thought, if the guy trailing me was worth his salt, I shouldn't be able to spot him. I continued to the top and finally reached Joe, who was standing with a young woman. And it wasn't Vanessa.

"Joe, where's Vanessa?" I asked out of breath.

"I'm ... Well ... you see, Jedi ..." I could tell Joe was searching for an explanation.

"Thanks for coming. My editor always likes to have at least two people in these kinds of pictures." The woman, who looked to be in her mid-twenties, had a camera draped around her neck.

"Excuse me. But what is going on?" I asked.

"Your friend didn't tell you?" she asked as she pulled off the lens cap.

"I was just about to. Really. You see, Jedi, Miss Capshaw works for the *Belltown News* and her assignment is to take some pictures of kids sledding but everyone is either sick of sledding or they're going to the carnival. So, I figured ..."

"That you'd tell me that I had a date with Vanessa so I'd get out of bed and pose for your pictures."

"Well ..." Joe shrugged his shoulders. He knew I was boiling.

"Joe, that's really cold. I can't believe you lied to me. I could, I could really..." I clenched my fist and headed down the hill.

Joe slid down after me "Jedi. Jedi. I'm really sorry but ..."

"But what?" I turned to him. "You lied to me. Friends don't lie to friends."

"So we're friends?" Joe smiled slightly.

"Yeah. Well, we were," I continued down.

"I'm sorry, Jedi. I shouldn't have lied to you. I just thought that if my picture was in the paper with you ..." He stopped and looked away.

"What, Joe?"

"Well, since you're popular and all and I only know a couple of year-round kids, it would kind of let everyone know that I'm all right." Joe was visibly embarrassed, and I have to admit, I was a little flattered.

"So can I take a picture of you guys or not?" Miss Capshaw yelled down. Joe waited for my answer.

"Don't ever lie to me again, Joe, especially when it deals with Vanessa." I looked at him long and hard.

"I swear on The Force." He made a sign with his fingers.

"OK, let's take some pictures." I smiled and realized it was very difficult to stay angry at Joe Clancy. For about ten minutes we went down the hill on Joe's sled and posed for different shots.

"Thanks guys. I just need your names. I know you're Joe Clancy and you're Jedi what?"

Joe and I both laughed.

"My name is Orville Jacques. Jedi is just a nickname."

"Oh, OK." She scribbled it down on her pad. "If you guys want the negatives just give me a call." She reached into her coat pocket and handed me her card—Eve Capshaw, Reporter, *Belltown News*.

"Excuse me, Miss Capshaw," I said.

"Please, call me Eve. I'm not that much older than you, Orville."

"OK, Eve. I was just wondering, if you're a reporter then why are you taking pictures of kids sledding?"

"Orville, I just got out of college. No offense to you guys, but you got to do a lot of boring stuff like this before they give you the big stories. I mean last week, they had me cover a church bake sale, a crosswalk being painted on Main Street, and a break-in."

"Well, the break-in was probably exciting," Joe said.

"If you're into bees."

"What?" we both asked.

"A beekeeper claimed someone broke into his special room where he has colonies and stole about two thousand bees."

"Why would anyone want to steal bees, especially in this weather?" I asked.

"I know, the beekeeper told me that they wouldn't survive very long this time of year except for in his screened room. Anyway, that's the kind of stuff that I'm doing," Eve said as she began to place the cap back on the camera.

"Wait, Eve, before you go, I want to show you something." Joe put his hand up to stop her and then he waddled behind some trees. She gave me a look of what's-going-on and I gave her a I-have-no-idea shrug. A minute later, Joe appeared holding a cardboard box that was about six feet tall.

"What is that?" Eve asked the question for both of us.

"My parents bought a new refrigerator and it came in this box."

"So?" I asked.

"So," Joe couldn't believe I didn't get it, "so this box will be awesome to sled in. Eve, can you take a picture of Orville and me sledding down in it?"

"Sure." She got her camera ready.

"Joe, don't even try talking me into this one. On this trip, you're flying solo."

"Like Hans Solo?" He smiled and crouched into the box, and began his journey before I could remind him that he wouldn't be able to see where he was going since he was inside the box. The box slid swiftly down the hill and began to veer to the left towards the baseball field's backstop.

"Uh, oh," Eve and I both said and followed with, "Jump out, Joe. Jump out!"

But our warning yells were futile. We both felt like we were witnessing a car crash and there was nothing we could do but watch in horror as the refrigerator box carrying Joe Clancy slammed into the backstop. When we got to the scene I expected the worst.

"Joe! Joe! Are you all right?" I shouted at the crumpled-up box. There was moaning for a couple of seconds finally followed by, "Yeah, I'm OK. Can you help me out?"

We pulled him out of the cardboard wreckage and he stretched a bit.

"I guess God punished me for lying to you, Orville." Joe nodded in thought.

I laughed in relief because he was OK.

"You're lucky you didn't break your neck!" Eve still had a worried look, but then the sound of a phone ringing interrupted us.

"Oh, that's my cell phone." She clicked it on. "Hello ... Yes ma'am ... I see." Eve's face lit up. "I understand ... No ... No ... Yes ... I can handle this story. I'll be right there. Thank you. I won't let you down. 'Bye."

"That sounds like good news," I stated, hoping she would fill us in.

"Guys, I think I'm going to have my first real byline. There's a press conference in an hour at the police station and my boss wants me to cover it."

"What's it about?" Joe asked. The pain was no longer in his face.

"Something was found on Breakers Beach last night. I only have an hour to get ready. See you guys later." She practically sprinted to her car.

"See you later," Joe and I both said. I knew "later" was only an hour away.

Joe and I settled in the back row of the police conference room and waited for the news conference to begin. I hadn't wanted Joe to come with me, but there was no choice in the matter. When Eve told us something was found at Breakers Beach, Joe's imagination ran wild with thoughts of pirate treasure. I couldn't burst his bubble and tell him that they had found a body so I just bit my lip and let him tag along. There were six people from the radio and news media. They were drinking coffee and chatting with each other giving their own theories of what was found. The room grew silent when Chief Sandford walked in. He placed a folder on the podium and tapped the microphone to check for sound.

"I decided to call a news conference so I wouldn't have to take five or six individual calls from you people. I want to clear the air now so the famous Belltown rumor mill won't start." Someone raised a hand interrupting the Chief.

"Excuse me, Miss?" the Chief said to the hand raiser.

"Eve Capshaw, *Belltown News*. Chief, I was wondering ..."

"Miss Capshaw," he spoke loudly into the mike, "is this your first news conference?"

"Yes sir," she nodded.

"Well, there is something you should know. I don't open the floor to questions until I give my statement. So, if it is OK with you, I'm going to give my statement now." The Chief glared down at her.

There were a few chuckles from two officers and the other reporters. They knew how tough the Chief was when it came to rookies, whether it be police, or in this case, reporters.

"OK. At approximately 4:42 this morning, Officer Jameson stopped at Breakers Beach to do his nightly check to make sure no homeless people were sleeping on the beach. At this time, he spotted something floating in the ocean. That is when he realized it was human remains."

I almost had to laugh at how they completely changed the story to keep my name out of the papers. The Belltown Police were sick of Orville Jacques but I didn't blame them. I was actually relieved. Exposure is one thing you don't want in my line of work. Chief Sandford went on and on about how Officer Jameson called backup and how quickly they responded. Just when I thought he wasn't going to give the media anything worth sinking their teeth into, he said, "A wallet was found in the victim's pants. In the wallet was the victim's driver's license. With that information we checked Missing Persons. The same name appeared. An autopsy was performed at seven o'clock this morning not only to find out the cause of death, but also to verify the age of the victim. We are now certain who it is: Nicholas Pushkin age 65. He lived on 22 Belltown Court. He was reported missing August 6th after he went out on his boat to fish. Now questions."

Eve raised her hand but the Chief pointed behind her. "Yeah, go ahead Ralph."

"What did the autopsy reveal as cause of death?" a short man asked as he gestured his pencil at the chief.

"Oh. I thought I mentioned that. It appears that Mr. Pushkin drowned. I looked at the weather report for August 6 and it was a horrible night to be out. Heavy rain and rough seas."

"Yeah, Candy." Again the Chief ignored Eve and pointed to Candy Carson, a local radio celebrity and long-time fixture in Belltown.

"Chief, I know everyone in this town. Well, at least, I

thought I did. Who was this Pushkin fellow? Can you give us any background information on him?"

Joe whispered in my ear, "Do you know this guy?"

"Never heard of him," I whispered back.

"From what we know, Mr. Pushkin moved from New York to Belltown about two years ago. He didn't have a wife or any children. He retired here to fish and enjoy the ocean."

"What did he look like?" Candy Carson was obviously agitated that she had no idea who this man was.

"We do have a picture of Mr. Pushkin, Candy, but it was taken about twenty years ago."

"I'd like to see it." She was determined.

"Officer Warner could you go get it? It's on my desk. Thanks. Yes, Tom." He pointed at still another reporter.

"Since Mr. Pushkin didn't have a family, who identified the body?" a man with horn rimmed glasses asked as he scribbled away.

"Look, I don't want this quote to get into the papers but as most of you would probably guess, there wasn't much to identify. But, we did have a friend of Mr. Pushkin's identify the clothing that Mr. Pushkin was wearing when he disappeared, and it was a perfect match."

"Who was the friend?" Tom fired the next question.

"He doesn't want his name in the papers."

Officer Warner came back into the room and handed the picture to the Chief, who held it up for the room to see—a man in his mid-forties with brown eyes, a floppy mustache, and a wide smile. "Joe, have you ever seen that guy around town?" I turned to Joe and his eyes were wide in amazement.

"Joe, what's wrong?"

"Ask them if Mr. Pushkin used to go to Licky's Ice Cream Store," he said softly.

"What?" I was confused.

"Just ask them," Joe demanded.

Even though it was a strange question, it meant something to Joe, and I was about to stand up and ask when Candy Carson beat me to it.

"I know that guy! He was a Russian man who used to hang out at Licky's. Boy, he looked a lot different twenty years ago. It must have been all that orange sherbet he ate. I think that was his favorite flavor." I turned to Joe but he was gone. All I saw was the door slam. I was going to follow when Eve finally spoke up. "Chief, are you going to let me ask my question or are we going to talk about our favorite flavors all day?" She was firm.

"Go ahead, Miss Capshaw. Give it your best shot."

"Well, why haven't you mentioned anything about the 911 call that came into the station at approximately 4:42 AM. this morning? Isn't that the real reason why Officer Jameson went to Breakers Beach?"

The Chief's smile was frozen and for the first time he was at a loss for words. "There was no ah, what ah, there was no ah, 911 call on our records."

"That's strange because I have a tape recording of the call right here." No one spoke as she pressed the button on her handheld tape recorder.

A female voice came first. "911. What is your emergency and where are you located?"

"I just pulled someone out of the water at Breakers Beach. And there's a body. There's a body. Breakers Beach."

Click. The man's voice sounded familiar but I couldn't place it. All hands shot up in the air, and the Chief's face had I'm-in-trouble written all over it. I really wanted to stay and watch the fireworks, but I couldn't help but think of Joe. I slipped out the back and headed out of the police station. Joe was sitting on a snowdrift wiping his eyes. I knew he had been crying.

"You knew Mr. Pushkin?" I asked softly.

"Yes, Jedi, but I knew him as Radar. I didn't know he was missing. I just thought he moved back to New York."

"Radar?"

"Yeah, he said that was his nickname. He was a really good guy. He'd lend me some money now and then so I could buy a Creamsicle."

I felt bad for Joe but at the same time I kept wondering why the CIA was investigating the drowning of a retiree who liked to fish and eat ice cream. It made no sense.

"I guess he loved orange sherbet," I said, trying to give Joe a memory to smile about.

"Yeah, but his favorite flavor was White Russian. He always told me that he liked the name and had a special love for it. I remember he would laugh and say, 'Maybe that's why I have such bad teeth.'" Joe gave a slight smile and then laughed. "Boy, were they bad."

"What do you mean? His teeth?"

"Yeah, he used to tell me if I didn't watch out I'd end up like him. The human jack-o'-lantern."

"The human jack-o'-lantern?" I didn't know what he meant.

"Yeah, that's what he called himself because every other tooth of his was missing so he looked like a jack-o'-

lantern. He didn't care, though. If he did, he would have worn dentures, but he told me he hated them."

The snapshot went off in my mind of the skull staring up at me. My heart gave that excited beat that only happens when I know something isn't quite right. I turned from Joe and closed my eyes and visualized the skull again smiling up at me. Yes, I could see it clearly now smiling up at me with a full set of teeth!

I was trying to sort everything out in my mind while sipping on my hot chocolate at Coffee Obsession. I figured the police had to have known that the body they found wasn't Nicholas Pushkin. Even the most bumbling cop wouldn't overlook the fact that the skeleton had all of its teeth, and Pushkin was the human jack-o'-lantern. So why did the police inform the public only a few hours later that Pushkin was the skeleton?

One word said it all to me—cover-up. That would also explain why they conveniently didn't have the 911 call in their records. How did Eve Capshaw acquire a recording of the call? That was a question I'd ponder another time. For now, I was thinking about the cover-up. I knew the Belltown Police helped in it, but I saw firsthand who was running the show—the CIA. What did they have to do with Nicholas Pushkin? And if the skeletal remains weren't Pushkin's, whose were they? And what do I do now?

"Jedi!" Joe waved his hand in my face to get my attention.

"Yeah, what?" I looked at him.

"You've been a zombie for five minutes now."

"Sorry."

"No problem. Are you gonna eat that cookie?" He licked his chops while staring at my chocolate chip cookie.

"Nah. Go ahead."

Joe reached over the table and accidentally kicked my foot.

"Sorry. I didn't mean to kick you." When Joe said that I thought of something Hilda had told me. If she hadn't accidentally brushed against my leg, she wouldn't have seen my future. If she hadn't touched me I'd still be worrying about that algebra test I had to make up for Mr. Reason and not some CIA cover-up. It must be tough for Hilda to have that kind of power to see someone's future by just touching them or their clothes, I thought. Joe grabbed the cookie and gobbled it up.

"Wait!" I said out loud.

"What?" Joe asked, dumbfounded.

"Nothing," I answered, but it was something. Even if Hilda doesn't touch a person, she still can have visions of them by touching a piece of their clothing. I thought of the small piece of black material from the skeleton that had jammed my coat zipper.

"What did I do with it?" I said softly. "That's right. It's in my wastebasket." I leaped from my chair.

"Where are you going?" Joe asked.

"I forgot I have to do some chores for my Mom. Here's a dollar. Buy a hot chocolate. On me." I rushed out the door before Joe could say anything. I had no idea what any of this was about. I knew the CIA was involved in it somehow and they had many secret weapons except for one—Hilda. I was hoping once she touched the black material, she would be able to tell me who the mystery skeleton really was.

Chapter Five

THERE WERE three people in front of Hilda's wagon waiting to have their fortunes told. I knew I couldn't just barge in front of them, so I was going to either have to wait about a half-hour or come back later. I decided on coming back later and began to walk away when a voice stopped me.

"Orville."

I turned around and Maxwell, the giant ticket-taker, motioned me to wait. I was a little stunned because it was the first time he called me by my name, and it wasn't in his threatening tone. He turned his attention back to the people who were waiting.

"The fortune-teller will be taking a half hour break after she's finished with the customer she's talking with now."

"Why didn't you tell us before we got in line?" a guy in his twenties asked, annoyed.

"I lost track of time. Come back in a half-hour." Maxwell didn't seem too concerned about their inconvenience. The three people left grumbling to themselves. A moment later, the door opened and the young customer appeared, smiling to herself as she walked away.

Maxwell pointed to the door. "OK, Orville. You can go in. She's been waiting for you."

"She's been waiting for me? Why?" I was intrigued.

"I don't know. Something she heard on the radio." He shrugged.

I nodded a thank-you and hopped the two steps. Hilda was standing inside the doorway.

"Orville, take a seat. I vill get tea. I have a fresh pot on. It should be ready by now." She disappeared behind the curtain. I sat down and leaned back in the chair.

"You know what I found this morning?"

"Yes," she said, "I heard it on the radio forty minutes ago."

"You don't sound surprised."

"Maybe I am. Maybe I am not. Maybe I am finally numb to all of the horrible things that my visions bring me." Hilda appeared holding a tray with the teapot and cups. As she poured she said, "The reporter said that this Pushkin fellow vas fishing, but the weather was so bad that his boat capsized. Maybe, some good at least came out of this vision. You found this man's remains and he can finally have a proper burial." Hilda handed me a cup.

"Thanks." I paused for a minute. "But I don't think that was Nicholas Pushkin who I found."

"But the police confirmed ..."

"Hilda, I saw the remains. The skeleton had all of its teeth. They used to call Pushkin the human jack-o'-lantern because most of his teeth were missing."

"Then if it is not Pushkin, who is it? And what happened to Pushkin?"

"That's why I'm here. I thought you could tell me."

I placed the small piece of black fabric on the table and Hilda stared at it.

"You told me sometimes if you just touch a person's clothing you can have visions. I got this piece of clothing off the skeleton."

"I do not know, Orville. If I touch that fabric I may not see anysing. But I might see somesing that could put you in great danger."

"Hilda, I don't understand. You have a wonderful gift to see things a normal person can't. Why don't you use that power to help?" I was agitated at her reluctance.

"A wonderful gift?" She slammed the cup down on the table, and it smashed to pieces causing me to jump and spill some of my tea.

"This is no gift. It is a curse. I did not ask to have this power you talk about. I had no choice." Hilda gave a deep sigh and then spoke softly as if she was telling me a bedtime story.

"My parents wanted a simple life so we moved from Hungary to America when I vas eleven years old. My father vas a tailor and mother vas a maid. It vas a simple, happy life until I vas thirteen. It all changed one day when my parents and I had a picnic. The beginning of the day was glorious, but it quickly became dark and the skies opened. It poured and we ran for cover under a tree. Then the lightning struck all three of us. When I woke, the doctor said my parents had died, and it was a miracle I was alive. He vas a kind man. I remember him saying, 'It will be all right little one.' It soothed me in a way, but when he gently touched my forehead with his hand, that soothing feeling became horror. I had a vision of him caught in a fire. I thought it may have been a bad dream but two days later, I heard some nurses whispering about the horrible tragedy. The doctor had died when his house burned down. I was thirteen years old. I didn't know any better. I thought I had caused it. So when I was well enough I ran away. I walked a busy city street and quickly realized I would never have a normal life again. When I brushed against shoulders of different people I saw some happy things like marriages, birthday parties, a boy hitting a baseball and people cheering. But most of the shoulders I brushed up against gave me frightful visions of a child dying of polio, a father dying in a car accident, or a mother dying of cancer. There vas nothing I could do but feel their pain and know I could not stop it." There was a lonely tear running down Hilda's cheek and she swatted it with her wrinkled hand.

"It is a curse, Orville, not a gift." She sipped her tea and composed herself.

"Then why did you become a fortune-teller?" I asked.

"When word got out of my visions, I vas considered a freak. Back in my day, they did not have one eight hundred numbers promoting psychics. People looked at me crazy. I tried to keep to myself never talking and that is why I still have my accent. But someone would find out my story and I was a freak again. The carnival people knew that same feeling of being considered abnormal, and they took me in. They made me part of their family and accepted me, knowing never to touch me. Do you know vhat it is like to be afraid to hug someone, knowing you might see a vision of how they will die?" She got up from her chair and poured more tea into my cup.

"I'm sorry, Hilda. I had no idea what you've gone through all of your life."

"It's OK, Orville. I did not mean to let my pain show in front of you, but for some reason, I feel like I can really talk to you." Hilda's eyes watered as she put the teapot down. I could see the pain now in her worn eyelids. She looked like she wanted to burst into tears, but she bit down hard on her lip.

"You can talk to me." I got up from my chair. She had the same look my grandmother had when Papa died, I thought. I wanted to comfort her, somehow, make that look go away, but I still hardly knew her. But something inside me told me to open my arms. I put them out to hug her. Her eyes widened like a frightened animal.

"It's all right, Hilda. I am not afraid of what the future brings me. So you shouldn't be either."

The dam broke in her eyes as she let me hug her, while she cried like a helpless child. It indeed reminded me of when Nana cried in my arms after she told me, "Papa has gone to heaven."

After Hilda let out her emotions she wiped her eyes dry.

"Orville, I cannot believe how good I feel. That vas the first time I've really cried in years."

"My parents say that crying is one of the emotions of life. So if you don't cry now and then you don't fully live."

"Your parents sound like wise people." Hilda sat back down and I nodded, yes.

She was quiet for a minute but then said, "I am ready, Orville. Hand me the material."

"I thought you didn't ..."

"I am ready," is all Hilda said as she shut her eyes and put her hand out. She rubbed the material in her hand for a couple of minutes as I watched, holding my breath.

"Yes. Yes. I see somesing. Oh, yes. I see two men fighting on a boat. The seas are rough and it is raining. Ah, um ..."

She rubbed the material again.

"One of the men has broad shoulders. I cannot make out his face. I can see the other man, though. He's bald. Gray mustache. Teeth. Yes, I see his teeth. He does not have many."

It had to be Pushkin, I thought. It had to be.

"I see. I see. The broad-shouldered man charges him but slips and falls overboard. I see water. Water. Yes, I see water. And. And then all I see is blackness." Hilda opened her eyes and said, "That is it."

"So Pushkin has to be alive unless he didn't survive the storm," I thought out loud.

"Yes." Hilda said as a knock interrupted us, "Who is it?"

Maxwell popped his head in, "Hilda, the same three people are back in line. I can't stall them any longer."

"OK, I'll be ready in a moment. Thank you, Maxwell."

"Hilda, I'm sorry I was hard on you."

"Orville, it is OK." She smiled brightly. "You helped me live a little today."

"One question, though. Why did you change your mind?"

"I might not tell you. But, someday I will let you know. And remember I vas smiling when I told you this."

Hilda was speaking in riddles, but I smiled and said, "I'll remember, Hilda. I'll remember."

Even though I had no clue what the cover-up was all about, I felt sure of two things—it had to deal with the CIA and Nicholas Pushkin. How were they connected? Two theories bounced around in my head as I trudged past Bill's Donuts. Either Pushkin was an agent for the CIA and they had him declared dead so he could take on a new identity and continue working for them, or they were after him for playing a part in the broad-shouldered man's death. Maybe the broad-shouldered man was a CIA agent, and that's why they were after him? That would be another reason why the CIA had the Belltown Police declare Pushkin dead. Pushkin might think he got away with it and come out of hiding—that is, if he wasn't hiding in the bottom of the ocean, waiting for a fish net to find him. I shuddered at the thought as I glanced over at the dumpster behind Bill's Donuts. I spotted Larry, the homeless man, putting soda cans in a bag. I wanted to ask him why he took off after we helped him at the carnival. I thought it had been kind of rude.

"Hey, Larry. What's up?"

Larry answered, "Nuthin'."

"Larry, I was wondering why you left us hanging with Officer Coughlin last night at the carnival?"

He looked up from his bag. "Sorry, I didn't want to get in trouble 'cause I didn't pay to get in."

"Oh, OK. I understand. See ya." All I wanted was an explanation so I began to walk away when he said, "Can you believe this?" His filthy hands held up a plastic soda ring made to hold six-packs.

"What about it?"

"These things are made for seagull hunting." Larry ripped the rings apart.

"Seagull hunting? No one hunts gulls on the Cape."

"Not on purpose. But people put these soda rings in the trash and they don't realize that if a gull picks through the garbage it could get its head caught in one of the rings, and snap!" he snapped his fingers, "broken neck. Dead gull. I hate to see dead gulls. 'Cause sea gulls are the Cape's angels looking down at us."

"I agree." And I did. I always thought there was something special about the gulls.

"Did you find your flashlight?" Larry asked as he went back to his work.

"Flashlight?"

"Yeah, I threw it by the dunes . . ." Larry poured out some soda from a near empty-can and flung it into his bag.

"Wait, Larry, you're the guy who pulled me out of the ocean this morning?"

"Yup."

"Why did you take off?"

"Sometimes I put my tent up on Breakers Beach. The cops have caught me a lot. They said the next time they catch me they're going to have me committed. So, I had to take off. Don't tell no one."

"Committed for just sleeping on the beach?"

"Well, they also think I'm nuts," he laughed, "but I don't have to tell you about my nickname—Looney Larry." He made a crazy face.

"Only a few stupid people call you that." I tried to brush over the subject. I have to admit though, sometimes Larry was out there and sometimes he was sharp as a tack. Many people didn't know what he suffered from. Some said he was a former boxer who was punch-drunk, others thought he was a war vet who was shell-shocked. On this day, he seemed to know what was going on, so I decided to ask him a couple of questions.

"When I walked out on the jetties, I saw fresh footprints. Did you see who made them?"

"That was me." He tied up his bag and then secured it to the back of his bike. I wondered how he was going to be able to ride his beat-up ten-speed on the poorly plowed streets.

"What were you doing on the jetties in the middle of the night?"

"I go out there sometimes to look at the UFOs." He didn't blink. He was serious.

"UFOs?" I raised my eyebrow.

"Yeah, unidentified flying objects. Now and then one appears for a couple of seconds in the middle of the night. But I haven't seen any in a few months," Larry said nonchalantly as he got on his bike.

"Oh, yea," I nodded, trying not to laugh.

"Thank your girlfriend and your little buddy for helping me last night." He began to peddle away.

"And thank you, Larry, for pulling ..." I couldn't finish. He turned the corner and disappeared like a flying saucer.

I called and asked my friend Gina to use her computer to try to find anything on Nicholas Pushkin. Gina had helped me before on cases and was always able to find something important. Not this time. She came up empty. I sat around my house that night stuck on the case and it didn't get any better Sunday morning. I read the paper but there was nothing worth noting except Eve Capshaw's first real byline titled "Police Deny Frantic 911 Call." It was a rehash of what I had witnessed in the conference room, and also how an unidentified source provided her a recording of the call. There was also a silly picture on page three of Joe and me sledding down the hill. My investigation had hit a roadblock, so I spent the rest of Sunday studying for my make-up test for Mr. Reasons and praying for more snow. There was talk of another 'big one,' but reality slapped me in the face Monday morning when my clock radio went off and the DJ said, "...a great song by The Samples. Now for the weather. We are going to get hit again but it won't start till around noon. So get up sleepyheads or you'll miss that big yellow school bus!"